SHINE

JODI PICOULT

SHINE

A short story

HODDER

First published in the United States in 2016 by Ballantine Books
An imprint of Penguin Random House, a division of Penguin Random
House LLC, New York

First published in Great Britain in 2016 by Hodder & Stoughton
An Hachette UK company

This edition published in 2017

1

A CIP catalogue record for this title is available from the British Library

ISBN 978 1 473 67289 5

Typeset in Sabon MT by Palimpsest Book Production Limited, Falkirk,
Stirlingshire

Printed and bound by Clays Ltd, St Ives plc

Hodder & Stoughton policy is to use papers that are natural,
renewable and recyclable products and made from wood grown in
sustainable forests. The logging and manufacturing processes are expected
to conform to the environmental regulations of the country of origin.

Hodder & Stoughton Ltd
Carmelite House
50 Victoria Embankment
London EC4Y 0DZ

www.hodder.co.uk

This year WHSmith celebrates its 225th anniversary and to mark this momentous occasion, we are pledging to raise £2 million split between three charities: Cancer Research UK, Mind and the National Literacy Trust.

Several authors have kindly agreed to supply WHSmith with exclusive short stories, in order to enable us to offer customers something new to the market and to donate £1 from each sale, split equally between the chosen charities.

We do hope you enjoy reading these specially chosen titles and join us in thanking the authors for their support.

Sandra Bradley
Trading Controller
Fiction Books

SHINE

September 1979

On the morning of Ruth Brooks's first day of class at the prestigious Dalton School, she sat in the kitchen of another family's house, waiting for her mama to finish packing her lunch. "You act like a guest," her mama instructed, spreading the same peanut butter on the same kind of bread that would be tucked into Christina's lunch, too. "You don't give them any reason to not invite you back."

In the past, Ruth had come only occasionally to the Hallowells' home, but all that was going to change. Now, every morning, Sam Hallowell's chauffeur would take her and Christina in a shiny black car through Central Park to the Upper East Side—91st Street—where she would be enrolled in third grade. At the end of the school day, she would return and play with Christina in her room or do homework in the kitchen until her mama finished working. Then they'd take the bus to Harlem, back to their own place, where Granny and Rachel would be waiting.

Ruth knew that it was a blessing to go to this fancy school. In first grade, she and her sister, Rachel, had both gone to a school that was mostly Orthodox Jewish kids. Ruth had loved it—everything from the snap-together cubes for counting to the felt board with a floppy sun, a listless cloud, a thunderbolt, a snowflake. But it was a two-hour commute each way on the bus. In second grade, Ruth had gone to public school in Harlem. It was as different from her first school as possible. There were no books in the school library that didn't have most of their pages ripped out. The teachers spent more time yelling than teaching. Rachel had never been an engaged student, but Ruth was having the life sucked out of her. She didn't know what conversation between Ms. Mina and Mama had led to this full scholarship, but she had taken a test and done well, and that was that—she was in. And she was grateful.

At least, she was supposed to be.

She swung her feet on the kitchen stool, thinking of Rachel, who didn't have to get up at 5:30 A.M. to go to school. Rachel was in fifth grade this year, and thought she knew everything. Like last night, she told Ruth that she would probably be the only Black girl in the whole school and nobody would talk to her. Ruth had asked her mama on the bus ride in whether that was true. "Ms. Christina will talk to you," her mama had said. "You two have known each other forever."

But there was a difference between visiting the brownstone on a random Saturday and playing with Barbies, and actually attending the same school as Christina. Plus, Christina had gone to this school since kindergarten and already had friends. Just thinking about it made Ruth's throat feel too tight.

Christina bounced into the kitchen. Her hair was caught back in her favorite barrette, the one with silk roses glued to it. She carried a spotless pink backpack.

"It's time to go," she said, her voice a musical scale. "You ready, Ruth?"

Ruth hopped off the chair. Her mama straightened her cardigan and handed her one of the bag lunches. "Baby girl," Mama said to Christina, "don't you forget this."

Christina took the matching lunch. As Ruth followed her into the parlor, Ms. Mina was waiting with little Louis in her arms. He was only three, not even in preschool yet, and he was not having a lot of success at potty training. "Are you excited, Ruth?" Ms. Mina asked. "First day!"

"Yes, ma'am," Ruth said. *Excited* and *terrified* felt as if they might be one and the same.

The sedan was already in front of the brownstone. The minute they walked outside, a man burst out of the car like a kernel of popcorn exploding. He opened the back door and gave

4

a little bow. "Ms. Christina," he said. "Ms. Ruth."

If Rachel could see this, she'd bust up. *Can't they open their own car doors?*

Ruth just said thank you and buckled herself in. She and Christina waved to their mothers on the stoop until they couldn't see them anymore. "Wait till you meet Lola," Christina said. "Lola has a pet monkey. I swear. It's part of her dad's work or something." She leaned toward Ruth. "It wears a *diaper*."

Ruth imagined going to a new friend's house and meeting this monkey in a diaper. She pictured teaching it a trick, like how to clap or something, and her new friend telling everyone else what Ruth had done.

And suddenly, they were there. The driver opened the door and Christina bolted from the car, shrieking and throwing her arms around a girl who had silvery blond hair. Lola, maybe? She didn't look back. They were talking so fast that it sounded like a different language.

The driver handed Ruth her backpack, which

had been Rachel's last year. "You have a nice day, Ms. Ruth," he said gently.

It was at that moment that Ruth realized her mother had never answered her *other* question on the bus: would there be anyone else at Dalton who looked like her?

Ruth stepped onto the curb. Then she took a deep breath and dove into a wave of white.

At Dalton you didn't get assigned to a teacher's classroom, you got assigned to a house—which, Ruth figured out quickly, was just a fancy word for a bunch of kids who were all the same age.

Christina was in her house, and so was the girl with the silvery hair—Lola. Ruth trailed them inside to Ms. Thomas's room, waiting for a break in the conversation so that she could introduce herself, like Mama told her to do. She waited for Christina to come to her rescue, to say, *This is Ruth*. But instead Christina ducked into the room and ran to the neat row of cubbies. "Lola," she called. "We're next to each other!"

Last year, Ruth had not had a cubby. She put

her lunch neatly in the bottom and hung her jacket up on a hook. When she turned around, there was a pretty redheaded lady crouched down, holding out her hand. "I'm Ms. Thomas," she said. "I'm the house adviser." Ruth guessed that was the Dalton word for *teacher*. "What's your name?"

"Ruth," she said.

"Well, Ruth, we are so glad to have you with us this year."

Ruth nodded. But she wondered who else Ms. Thomas was speaking for; who was the *we* in that equation.

They played a game where everyone clapped a rhythm that went with their name, and everyone else in the class had to mimic it. Ruth tapped her right knee, left knee, then waved her hands like she was singing hallelujah at church. *Ruth,* everyone said, and they did the same motion she had done. It made her think of her granny's story about going to the French part of Canada once, and how she had to do charades just to ask where the toilet was.

7

Ms. Thomas wore a double strand of pearls that had a glittery spider clasp in the back, and Ruth counted the number of times that the spider slipped down her neck and Ms. Thomas had to tug it back into place. Ms. Thomas showed everyone a picture of herself in a white princess dress, with a handsome man beside her in a tuxedo. It looked like snow was falling on them, but it was rice. She told everyone that her husband's name was David and then she showed another picture, this one of a very small dog called Caesar. "That's my family," she said. "Now I want you to draw me a picture of yours!"

Ruth was placed at a table with a boy named Marcus (clap up high, clap down low) and a girl named Maia (tiny claps all around her face, like the petals of a sunflower). Ruth had seen Marcus pick his nose during the circle time, and between that and the fact that he was a boy, she had very little interest in him. Maia, though, was the only other student in the house who was new to Dalton. She had moved from Dallas.

She had red hair like a molten river that was held back by a rhinestone headband. She had an accent, and when she spoke, her voice was full of music.

At each seat was the kind of thick vanilla drawing paper Ruth remembered from her year at the Jewish school. A confetti of crayons splashed the center of every table. "We have to share," Maia announced. She took the crayons and rolled a few toward each of them, divvying up the colors.

Christina was all the way across the room. Ruth wondered what she was drawing to illustrate her family, whether Mama would be part of it. After all, Mama spent more hours taking care of Christina than her own mother did; it was her job. And Ms. Mina was always calling Mama *family*. But could Mama be on Christina's drawing *and* Ruth's? Didn't Ruth get first dibs?

Or what if Christina left Mama out of her drawing? Did that suggest family meant different things to different people?

Honestly, Ruth couldn't figure out what would make her more upset: seeing Christina's finished drawing with Mama in it, or not.

"You get these," Maia announced, pushing a bunch of crayons toward Marcus and another group toward Ruth.

"No way," he said. "I need flesh color." He grabbed the peach crayon that was in front of Maia.

Ruth looked at the crayons in front of her. She picked up the dark blue, because Maia had saved the black for herself. She made the outline of Mama, and then drew in Rachel and herself and Granny. Then she picked up the brown crayon.

Marcus was coloring in his family with the peach crayon. Maia was making a big deal of having to wait for it.

Ruth colored her mother's face. She forgot to leave white for the eyes, and couldn't go backward, which left Mama looking angry. So she was more careful as she drew her own face. She touched the brown crayon gently to the page, shading so faintly she could barely see the pigment.

Recess happened on the roof of the school building, an artificial garden in the middle of the city. Maia had drawn the girls in the house to her like filings to a magnet. She told them that in Texas she had lived on a ranch and ridden horses every day, something New York City girls did only during summer camp and something Ruth had never done. Horses frightened her. She didn't like the yellow of their huge teeth.

She took a deep breath and sat down just behind Christina, as if she were about to start a second concentric circle, even if she was the only member. Christina glanced over her shoulder and then scooted to the right, creating a few inches of space that couldn't fit Ruth's leg, much less her whole body. Maia was designing some sort of game: "And this is the castle, and the boys over there are the trolls that can't ever touch you, and if you cross the line by the bench you're out of the whole kingdom, and—"

Ruth wedged her feet into the spot Christina had created and scooted as far forward as she could. "Can I play too?"

Maia stared at her and scrunched her nose. "But we're playing *Princess*," she said. "You can't be a princess. You don't have the right hair."

Instinctively, Ruth touched her hair. It curved in a bob to just above her chin. Lola touched it. "I like your hair," she said. "It's pretty."

"My granny used the hot comb," Ruth said, and all six girls in the circle looked at her blankly.

Ruth puffed up a little, excited to know something they didn't. "Yeah," she continued. "You heat it up on the stove, and while it's getting ready Granny puts green Super Gro grease on my hair, and then when the comb's really hot, she runs it through to get it all straight."

Lola stared at Ruth. "And it just stays like that?"

"Yeah. Till she washes it again in a couple of weeks."

Maia's eyes widened. "You don't wash your hair every day?" she said. "Do you even *shower*?"

The others girls laughed. Ruth couldn't see Christina's face, couldn't hear whether she was laughing, too. She felt tears cutting the tunnel of her throat, and stood up fast, her fists at her sides. "I don't want to play your game," Ruth said, and she looked down at Christina. "You want to go over there and play something else?"

Christina hesitated. She looked up at Ruth, but her eyes weren't full of *I'm sorry*. They were angry, as if she blamed Ruth for making her the rope in this tug-of-war. Christina ducked her head without answering.

Ruth ran to the far corner of the rooftop garden. She lay down on the ground, staring up at the clouds so that it was easy to think that they weren't even in the city anymore, if you blocked out the sound of the car horns from below. She blinked fast, and kept her eyes extra wide, and all the other tricks she knew to keep from crying.

She could hear Maia assigning character names. Princess Marigold. Princess Daffodil. Princess Ivy.

Ms. Thomas walked toward Ruth and sat down beside her, following Ruth's gaze up to the sky. "You know," she said, as if they had been in the middle of a conversation, "there are stars there right now. You can't see them, because they're obscured by the sun. But the minute the sun goes away, wow—they're as bright as jewels."

Ruth didn't know why Ms. Thomas was telling her this. She didn't know why Ms. Thomas had come over here in the first place. She just wanted to go home. She wanted to be in Harlem in school with Rachel. Except she didn't really want to be there, either. So where did that leave her?

"Can I tell you a secret?" Ms. Thomas whispered. "We're going to study stars this year. But I'm trusting you not to tell anyone else, all right? It's going to be a surprise."

Ruth sat up, hugging her knees to her chest. "Deal?"

"Yes, ma'am," Ruth said.

Ms. Thomas put her arm around Ruth's shoulders and squeezed. "Would you be the leader for me today, when we line up to go downstairs?"

Ruth nodded.

Ms. Thomas stood up and clapped. "Okay, boys and girls! Line up behind Ruth!"

Ruth stood at the door that led into the building and down the stairs. She thought about the secret Ms. Thomas had told her. She liked holding on to it. Sometimes at Ms. Mina's she took a hard candy from the bowl in the foyer and kept it in her pocket and didn't eat it, because she liked to stick her hand inside hours or even days later and know she had a surprise nobody else had.

"Everyone line up behind Ruth," Ms. Thomas repeated, and Ruth stood a little taller.

On the bus that night, headed back home, Mama wanted to know everything: What were the names of the friends she made? What did she learn in school? What was her teacher like?

Ruth told her about the clapping game and Marcus picking his nose and how she got to be the recess leader.

"And what about the other girls?" Mama asked.

"There's Maia," Ruth replied. "She's from Texas and she used to ride horses every day. We played Princess during recess."

Mama smiled so wide Ruth could see the pink of her gums. "Isn't that fine," she said.

It was the first time, Ruth realized, that she had ever lied to her mama.

But then, was it so bad to lie if you told someone what you knew they needed to hear?

The amount of freedom at Ruth's new school was staggering. As long as you weren't making trouble, you could just get up and go to the bathroom, without raising your hand first. There were breaks and free periods and recess and times when students were working on individual projects. Even in third grade, the Dalton administration believed, children could and should choose their own paths.

Ruth's path was unobtrusive. She stuck close to Christina, if Christina let her—which was usually when no one else was around. Maybe out of guilt and maybe out of kindness, when Maia and the others *did* show up, Christina made sure that Ruth was still included, even if it meant just tagging along with the rest of them and laughing when the others laughed, although she hadn't heard the joke. Maia was the sun and they were all in orbit; Ruth happened to be on the outskirts of the universe.

Maia's birthday was the second Friday of school, and her mother brought in cupcakes. Each one had a maple leaf poking out of the icing. The leaf was translucent, made of sugar, and was painted with some kind of edible paint so that it looked real. Ruth had never seen anything like it, and she wanted to show her mother and Rachel, so she carefully wrapped hers in a paper towel and tucked it into the pocket of her sweatshirt.

Because it was Maia's birthday, she was the leader of the recess line that day. Everyone fell into place behind her, snaking down the hallway. From her vantage point farther back in the line, Ruth could see that Maia was wearing her sparkling rhinestone headband. But now, Ruth realized, there were three other girls in the class who had matching ones. They looked like halos.

Ruth turned away and focused her attention instead on the bulletin board that was on the wall. Ms. Thomas had hung up the family portraits they'd drawn on the first day of school, which felt like a thousand years ago. It was easy for Ruth to find hers, because it was the only picture with brown faces.

Well, actually that wasn't true. Ruth let her eyes hopscotch over the other drawings until she found Christina's. There was Christina, front and center, with Ms. Mina and Mr. Sam. There was her little brother, Louis. And in the far right corner, much smaller than the other bodies, was a brown woman wearing an apron and holding a plate of cookies. Ruth knew it was supposed to be Mama. Her mama floated there like an untethered astronaut.

Ruth imagined her swimming off the edge of Christina's page, across the bulletin board, and settling into Ruth's drawing, where she belonged.

Ruth felt a shove in her back and realized that while she had been busy daydreaming the line had started moving. Ruth muttered an apology to Lola, who stood behind her, and hurried to catch up to the others.

To be honest, Ruth had never really thought about the fact that her mama had to cook dinner for Christina's family and then come to Harlem and cook all over again for her own. Maybe it was Christina's drawing that got her thinking about this, but that night at home, she found herself watching Mama cook chicken in the pan. As usual, Granny was dozing in front of the TV; she helped out where she could but that was less and less as she got older. "Mama?" she asked. "Don't you get sick of doing everything twice?"

"What do you mean, baby?"

"You have to take care of Christina's house and our house too," Ruth said.

Her mama smiled. "Well, now," she replied. "One I do for work. The other I do for love."

Just then Rachel walked into the kitchen and snorted. "It's still double the dishes," she said.

Mama gave her a sharp glance. "Then maybe you should start doing your share of chores?"

It was at that moment Ruth remembered the maple leaf candy. "I have something to show you," she announced. "They were on top of Maia's birthday cupcakes."

She dug her hand into her sweatshirt pocket and unwrapped the paper toweling. The leaf, however, had broken into pieces, some so fine they'd turned themselves back into granulated sugar.

"What's that?" Rachel asked.

"A leaf made of candy," Ruth answered.

"Okay." Rachel laughed. "If you say so."

After dinner, Mama told Rachel to take Ruth with her to play outside so she could sit down with

Granny in the living room and put her feet up for a hot second. Ruth sat on the curb while Rachel and two of her friends giggled over the older boys shooting hoops in the lot across the street. "You see Joziah?" Denyce said. "He all that."

Nia popped a bubble with her gum. "I heard he's strapped."

"What?" Rachel said. "That's wack."

Sometimes it seemed to Ruth that Rachel and her friends spoke a different language.

"He ain't got no gun," Denyce said. "He just like to tell people he do."

A gun? Ruth didn't realize she'd spoken out loud until the girls all stared at her. "Oh, look," Nia said. "We shocked your baby sister."

If Mama knew Rachel was anywhere close to the boys in this neighborhood who got into trouble, she would whup her and keep her locked inside.

"Leave me alone, Nia," Ruth said. "I'm not bothering you."

Nia smirked. "So what you sayin'?"

"Hey, Ruth," Denyce asked. "How's your

fancy school?" She got up from the stoop and sat down next to Ruth. Nia followed suit, sandwiching her on the other side.

"Look at that," Nia said, grabbing Ruth's wrist. "I think your skin's getting lighter."

"You practically a ghost," Denyce said, and both girls broke up laughing.

"Aight, you fools," Rachel interrupted. "Leave her be. It ain't her fault she smarter than both your brains put together."

"I'm going inside," Ruth announced, but she was pretty sure no one cared.

Her mama and Granny were on the couch, watching *Wheel of Fortune*. "What's the matter, baby?" Mama asked.

"Nothing," Ruth said. "I just wanted to take a bath."

She went into the bathroom the four of them shared. The tub had a crack in it that was the shape of a lightning bolt, and Ruth used to think that the water would run right through Mrs. Nattuck's ceiling, but since she'd never complained and they bathed every night, that probably wasn't the case. She ran the water and put on a shower cap to cover her hair and sank down to her shoulders. Then she lathered up soap on her washcloth. Her palms were pink, as pink as Christina's. She flipped her hand over, to the light brown of her wrist and forearm. Her skin had always been lighter than Rachel's; her sister had been dark as a berry her whole life. Was that why Ruth was the one who was going to Dalton?

Ruth picked up the washcloth and scrubbed at her left shoulder. She scrubbed so hard she could see the pink bloom of irritation under the brown of her skin.

It hurt.

It was beautiful.

On Monday, Ruth woke up before her alarm. She had brushed her teeth and dressed and packed up her schoolwork before her mama even came out of her bedroom. "Isn't someone in a hurry!" Mama said, but she smiled.

Ruth couldn't wait to get back to Dalton.

Today they would be playing a math game and the winning team would get Halloween candy. She had practiced her times tables all weekend. She would win, and then she would share the candy with Maia and the other girls, and this time they would not just tolerate her, they'd welcome her.

When they reached Ms. Mina's brownstone and went in the service entrance, Ruth raced up the stairs. She sat on a kitchen stool, kicking her legs, and printed out multiplication equations on a napkin. Ms. Mina came into the kitchen for a cup of coffee. "It's just finished brewing," Mama said. "I would have brought it up to you."

"Oh, I know that, Lou," she answered. "I was up all night with the baby and my body simply couldn't wait another second." She glanced at Ruth, who was now solving her equations. "Well, look at *you*!" Ms. Mina said. "And I can barely get Christina out of bed!"

But this wasn't true because at that moment Christina came into the kitchen, wearing a rhinestone headband, to pick up her school lunch from Mama.

There were two teams. Ms. Thomas randomly divided the students in half, and set up a buzzer on a desk in the middle of the classroom. One member of each team would face off as she recited a multiplication equation. The first person to hit the buzzer and say the correct answer would get to shoot a ball made of masking tape into one of three baskets. The farthest one was worth the most points. At the end of the game, the team with the most points would win.

Ruth faced off against Marcus first, and was given a cream puff of a question: 3 x 4. She rang the buzzer and tossed the tape ball into the trash can that was closest, because she didn't want to risk missing completely and they were better safe than sorry. They rotated through two more times, and each time, Ruth won her heat (6 x 6, and the very tricky 8 x 9). Maia was on the other team, along with Christina. Ruth knew it wasn't charitable, but when Maia screwed up and said 4 x 7 was 24, her stomach flipped with satisfaction.

Finally it was tied, and Ms. Thomas said they had to choose a designated shooter from each team to make a winning basket. It would be sudden death—the person who was picked would throw the tape ball and then the opposing team's pick would do the same, until one of them missed. Ruth leaned back against the wall, waiting for her team to rally around Edward or Lucas, who were the most athletic in the class. But instead, someone suggested her name.

At first, she flushed with pride—was she being chosen because her team recognized her as an MVP? But then she realized that wasn't what was going on here. "Yeah, Ruth," Edward said, nodding. "You know how to play basketball, don't you?"

Ruth nodded. She did know *how*—she'd watched neighborhood kids for years. But she'd never actually played the game herself.

"Of *course* she does," said Lucas. "Duh."

Reluctantly, Ruth took the tape ball and sank a basket into the farthest trash bin. Her team shouted and Lucas even gave her a high five.

The designated shooter for the other team was a tall boy named Jack who stuck out his tongue when he was concentrating, which wasn't often. He narrowed his eyes and let the tape ball roll off his fingertips. He, too, made the farthest basket.

Ruth took the ball again. She was not an athlete. She could barely walk and sing simultaneously during the Christmas pageant at church. There was absolutely no way she could be lucky enough to succeed a second time around. Then she remembered how Mama said there was no such thing as luck, just prayers being answered. So even though Ruth was certain God had more important things on His mind, she called on Jesus under her breath, and made a second basket. A third. Her teammates went wild. *Water into wine? Ha,* Ruth thought. This newfound athletic skill was a true miracle.

Jack took the ball, bounced on the tips of his toes, and stuck out his tongue. He arched one arm up, but the tape got snagged on the cuff of his sweater and fell about six feet short of the closest trash can.

"We have a winner!" Ms. Thomas sang, above a chorus of *Do over!* and *Not fair!* Ruth's team was hollering, patting her on the back and the shoulder, shouting her name. The teacher took out a bag of candy—Reese's peanut butter cups and Nestlé Crunch bars and Gobstoppers—and everyone on Ruth's team was allowed to stick their hand in and take a fistful.

Ruth made sure she got extra Reese's, then walked to Christina's desk. Maia was sitting on the top of it, whispering to Christina. "Want some?" Ruth asked, and she held out her cupped hands, letting them choose first.

"Everyone knows why you won," Maia said.

Ruth lifted her chin a notch. "Because I knew my times tables."

"More like because of how you look." Maia tossed her hair. "I don't want your dumb candy," she said, and she walked away.

Ruth stared at her. Christina fished through the candy Ruth held, choosing a Reese's. She unwrapped it and took a bite of the candy, leaving little ridges in the wake of her teeth. "I knew my times tables," Ruth murmured.

"It's not you, Ruth," Christina said. She popped the rest of the candy into her mouth. "She just doesn't like Black people."

Ruth watched her granny's hands twist Rachel's hair, pulling and crisscrossing to magically create the neat cornrows that weaved across her scalp in parallel zigzags. Rachel winced and whined, like always, but the end result was the same: tight, even braids that fell down to her shoulders. "Done," Granny pronounced, holding up the big hand mirror so that Rachel could see the back. "Ruth?"

Every other Sunday night, Granny washed and styled her granddaughters' hair. Granny had run her own place for years before it got to be too much for her to stand on her feet all day. Ruth climbed onto the stool, her hair still damp under the towel.

Granny's hands rooted through Ruth's hair, her fingernails scraping the scalp in a massage. She took her comb and made the first part.

"Wait—can you put the hood thing on and use the hot comb instead?" Ruth blurted out. "Please?"

Granny laughed, her hands on her wide hips. Ruth had always thought her granny looked like the sail of a ship—heavy-masted, wide, implacable. "Lou, you hear this? Queen of Sheba here wants a press."

Mama, who was sewing a button onto one of Ruth's white school shirts, looked up from where she sitting at the kitchen table. "You should be grateful your granny's doing *anything* to your hair," she said. "We're not running a salon."

Granny was pulling tighter on her hair. "Ain't never had no complaints before from my own grandbaby . . ."

30

"It's not you," Ruth said, hearing Christina's words beneath her own. "It's that I want to look more . . . grown up."

What she wanted was to look like Maia, with her river of shining hair. But that was about as likely as Ruth waking up in a millionaire's penthouse. Granny and Mama exchanged a look, and then Mama shrugged.

"Fine," Granny sighed. "Go get the comb."

Ruth scrambled to the cabinet where they kept the bonnet dryer and hot comb. Granny set the drying cap over her head and then placed the comb on the metal coil of the stove. After the bonnet cut off, she ran the Super Gro through a section of hair. Ruth tried not to think about how she had explained this to the other girls; how they had looked at her like she was an alien.

She held still as Granny ran the comb through her hair; she'd been burned enough to know the consequences of fidgeting. By the time she was finished, Mama had mended two more shirts, let out one of Rachel's skirts ("That girl

31

grows like a weed," she muttered), and darned a sock. Rachel walked into the kitchen to get an apple out of the refrigerator and looked at Ruth. "You goin' somewhere special?" she asked.

"Just school."

"It looks good," Rachel said, as Ruth narrowed her eyes, suspicious. "Like that skater lady. Dorothy Hamill."

"For real?" Ruth asked.

Rachel took a bite. "Nope," she said.

"Rachel!" Mama warned, but her sister was already cruising out of the kitchen on a laugh.

"Don't you listen to her, baby," Granny said. "You beautiful, inside and out."

She held up the mirror so that Ruth could see both the front and the back. Her hair was straight and shiny, curving just slightly at the bottom. "You know what would make this even more perfect?" Ruth said. "A headband."

"So go get a headband," Granny said. "You got that nice red one you wore at Easter."

"Some of the girls in my class have the kind

that sparkle," Ruth said, as casually as she could manage. "I wish I had one."

Mama didn't even look up from the sock she was mending. "We're not made of money, Ruth," she said, and she bit off the thread with her teeth.

On Columbus Day, Dalton was closed, but Mama still had to work. Rachel was invited to Nia's apartment and Ruth tagged along to the Upper West Side to play with Christina. Since Mr. Sam was out, Christina had Mama set up his movie projector, so that she and Ruth could watch the *Wonderful World of Disney* films that lined his shelves in their round metal tins. He worked in television, and their house was full of treasures Ruth could appreciate, like that, and others she couldn't—like the framed, signed photographs of movie stars she didn't know: Doris Day, Jack Lemmon, Steve McQueen.

Ruth and Christina ate grilled cheese sandwiches and tomato soup that Mama had made, and watched *Cinderella*. Christina was the only person Ruth knew who could watch a movie in her house and not have to go to a movie theater. They sat on Mr. Sam's red leather couch and shared an afghan that Ms. Mina had knitted when she was going through a crafty phase.

When the prince kissed Cinderella at the end, Christina said, "You know, it doesn't just work like that."

"Like what?"

"Like you can marry a prince if you're some nobody. You have to have a title."

Ruth thought about this. "Like a book?"

"I don't know," Christina admitted. "But not everyone has one. Maia said."

Maia said. Of course. "Does *she* have a title?" Ruth asked.

Christina considered this. "Bossypants?"

A surprised laugh bubbled out of Ruth. Then Christina was laughing, too, and it was the two of them and no one else, like it used to be.

Christina turned to her when the projector started flapping, the film having run its course.

"Now what should we do?" she said. "Want to see my new Malibu Barbie?"

We. Was there a better word in the English language?

"Christina?" Ruth said hesitantly. "This is fun, right?"

Christina looked at her sidelong. "Yeah, weirdo," she said, grinning.

"So when we're at school, then . . . are you mad at me?"

There was a pause. "No," Christina said, but in that hiccup of time, Ruth heard a thousand yeses. "Why would you even think that?"

"Because you act different when it's not just us."

"No I don't!"

"You do," Ruth said, but now she was second-guessing herself. Was she imagining it? Christina had been nothing short of nice all day. Maybe the problem wasn't Christina, but Ruth herself. It wasn't like it was Christina's job to defend Ruth from Maia; Ruth had to do that on her own. So why was she blaming Christina?

Suddenly she realized Christina was crying. "Why are you being so *mean* to me?" she said, just as Mama walked in to take away their empty plates.

"Christina?" Mama said, alarmed. She crouched down and gave Christina a tissue from her own pocket to dry her face. "What happened?"

"I don't want to play anymore," Christina sobbed, red-faced, not even looking at Ruth.

"Okay, then, you go on up to your room, and I'll bring you some dessert. I baked fresh blondies. That sound good to you?"

Christina sniffled and nodded, and a minute later, she was gone. Mama folded her arms. "What did you say to upset Ms. Christina?"

The truth? Ruth thought. But instead she lowered her eyes. "Christina's only my friend when we're here," she confessed. "The minute we walk through the door of school, everything changes."

She expected Mama to get mad at her for lying. After all, it had been nearly six weeks and Ruth had gone on and on about how great school was, how many friends she had made. But instead Mama sighed and took Ruth's hand. "Baby girl," she said, "*nothing* changes."

Two days later, Ms. Thomas got a student teacher. Miss Van Vleet was in college and would be coming to their classroom only on Tuesday and Thursday mornings. She would help the students who needed extra work with their writing, and she would be teaching some of the lessons. But that first day, her main job was to learn everyone's name, and she was really, really bad at it.

She called Maia *Mara,* and Lola *Lulu.* She mixed up Edward and Lucas.

Ms. Thomas tried to help her by giving her a stack of graded papers to hand out after recess. Miss Van Vleet wandered around the classroom, sometimes asking other students for help. Some of the boys tried to confuse her as a prank, and after that, when she had a question, she went straight to Ms. Thomas.

"Which one is Ruth again?" Miss Van Vleet asked.

Ms. Thomas looked up from where she was marking papers. She glanced around the room to see where Ruth was sitting, and Ruth met her gaze. Instead of pointing, she turned to Miss Van Vleet and hesitated for a moment. Then she said, "She's the girl with the red sneakers."

Ruth looked down at her red Keds. There were three other girls in her classroom who had the same shoes.

On the other hand, she was the only Black student.

That night, Rachel was being grounded without television privileges because she'd decked a girl for stealing her HoHos at lunch. That punishment wouldn't have bothered Ruth, who would have happily sat in her room reading, but Rachel had never willingly picked up a book, as far as Ruth could remember. So instead, while Ruth tried to memorize words for her spelling test, she had to block out the sound of Rachel galumphing around the room they shared, trying to find some other way to occupy her time.

"You want me to test you?" Rachel offered.

"Why?"

There was probably a catch. With Rachel, there was always a catch. It wasn't that she didn't love her sister; it was just that they saw the world through two different lenses.

"Because I'm being nice. And because I'm bored as all get out." She reached out her hand, and hesitantly Ruth gave her the list of words. Rachel climbed onto her bed and stuffed a pillow behind her head. "Baby words," she muttered, reading them over. *"Means."*

"M-E-A-N-S."

"Corn."

"C-O-R-N."

"Argue."

"A-R-G-U-E."

"This is stupid," Rachel said. "You don't even have to try. Why doesn't your teacher bump you up a level?"

Ruth didn't know the answer to that; there were other students who had more challenging words, although she had never gotten less than a 95 on a spelling test.

"Well, *I* know why, even if you don't," Rachel said. "Because your teacher doesn't think a Black girl can be at the top of the class."

"That's not true," Ruth immediately said, defending Ms. Thomas. "She knows I'm smart."

"Uh-huh," Rachel answered, in a way that meant anything but that.

"She doesn't even see me as Black," Ruth countered.

Rachel laughed. "Yeah, 'cause she's too busy seeing you as a charity case."

Ruth knew that her sister meant this as a dig, but she fiercely believed that Ms. Thomas saw more than just her skin color. She saw a girl who always said please and thank you and who never interrupted someone else if they were talking. She saw a student who was one of the best readers in the class, who loved learning astronomy. She saw a good listener, a willing friend.

She saw someone who was one of them.

Smugly, Ruth told Rachel what had happened that day at school. How Ms. Thomas had identified her.

"You really think the reason she pointed you out by your sneakers was because it was the only thing she could use to describe you?" Rachel asked.

That was all it took—that chink in the foundation, that worm of a question—for Ruth to peek behind the fancy wrapping of the story she'd created in her own mind. The justification, the wishful thinking—it was swept away by the broom of doubt like so much smoke.

Ruth knew she was partly right: Ms. Thomas had been showing a kindness by not singling Ruth out for her appearance. She was trying to be inclusive by not calling Ruth "the Black girl."

But that was because to Ms. Thomas, to

Maia, to Miss Van Vleet—to everyone in that school—Black wasn't just any adjective.

It was something they'd never want to be.

"I know you don't want to be my friend," Ruth said by way of prefacing her conversation with Christina in the sedan on the way to school. "But can I ask you something?"

For almost a week now, they had moved in similar orbits, but they had not interacted unless they were forced to in a group project. Christina didn't look at Ruth, but she jerked her chin: *Okay.*

Ruth explained what had happened with Ms. Thomas and Miss Van Vleet. "If you were in a crowd with a lot of people and someone asked me who you were, I wouldn't say you're the one with the scar on your ankle from where you fell last summer. I'd use something everyone would see right away, like . . . your purple shirt or your Holly Hobbie lunch box. Doesn't it seem weird?" Ruth asked. "To not call something what it *is*?"

Christina didn't answer, and Ruth thought it was because she was still mad at her. But then she turned in her seat so that she was facing Ruth. "Maybe no one notices that you're Black," she said. "I mean, you act and sound just like *we* do."

Ruth thought about this. It couldn't really be true, could it? If she dressed in pants and played baseball and did gross things that boys did, like have burping contests, would teachers not know that she was a girl? You couldn't *unsee* what was right before your eyes, could you?

Before she could mull on this further, Christina spoke again. "I never said I didn't want to be your friend," she said, her voice small. "It's just . . . all of a sudden you're at *my* school, with *my* friends, and I thought . . . I thought . . ." She raised her hand to the window and spread her fingers like a starfish. "What if they liked you more than they like me?"

Ruth didn't know what to say. It was the first time she realized that a person might look like Christina, and live in a fancy home, and dress in designer clothing, and have everything her heart desired, and still go to sleep at night worrying.

Maybe we are *more alike than we're different*, Ruth thought.

When Ms. Thomas turned off the lights in the classroom, everyone got quiet. Then she flicked them back on again. "Now," she asked, "how long did it take for the light to come back?"

It was instantaneous, immediate. There was probably a word for faster-than-a-heartbeat but Ruth didn't know it.

"Light moves fast. It can move 186,000 miles per second," Ms. Thomas said. "The reason it seems like we see light the instant I turn on the switch is because light is so quick, and because we're so close to it. But some light comes from much farther away—light from stars. They're so far away, in fact, that we don't even measure the distance in miles. We measure it in light-years—the amount of time it takes for light from that star to reach us, on earth. The reason stars look so small in the night sky is because they're so far away from us."

Ms. Thomas talked about the star that was closest to earth—the sun. She made Marcus stand at the front of the class with a flashlight and told him to turn it on. "If he was on the sun, and turned on a very bright flashlight . . . and we were all waiting in the classroom, we wouldn't see that light for eight minutes. *That's* how far away the sun is from us." The next closest star was called Proxima Centauri. It was 39.9 trillion kilometers away from us, or 4.2 light-years, which meant that it would take four years—not just eight minutes—for Marcus's flashlight to reach us on earth from there.

Ms. Thomas said that when we look at a star, we're looking backward in time. We're seeing a moment that happened millions of years ago.

Ruth thought about that. She knew Marcus's little flashlight wasn't powerful enough, but even so. What if there were kids on another planet who, years from now, saw it flash? What if, in the future, they had a piece of the moment Ruth was living right now?

It made her feel like yesterday and tomorrow weren't all that far away from each other.

Then Ms. Thomas gave everyone a toilet paper roll and a circle of black paper. Each student could choose to create either the Canis Major constellation or Orion. Ruth looked over and saw Maia pick Orion. She reached for the other one.

They had to trace the spiky limbs of the constellations, and poke tiny holes in at their joints to make the stars. Ruth carefully drew the T of Canis Major, and its split legs. It looked to her like a stick figure without a head. She used a pin carefully to mark the stars. Then with Ms. Thomas's help she affixed the black circle to one end of the roll, with electrical tape to seal the edges. When everyone in the class had finished, Ms. Thomas gave each of them a small penlight and pulled the drapes shut and turned off the classroom fluorescents. Everyone lay on the floor, shining their penlights through the toilet paper rolls, projecting their constellations onto the ceiling.

Ruth felt someone lie down beside her, and she turned to find Ms. Thomas staring up at the ceiling. "You see that star in the middle on top?" she asked, pointing, and Ruth nodded. "That's called Sirius. It takes light from that star eight and a half years to reach us here."

"That's how old I am," Ruth said.

"Well, then." Ms. Thomas laughed. "If you can see it in the night sky, you're looking at light that's the same age as you."

Ruth liked the idea of a star that she had something in common with. She wondered if she could convince her mother to let her out on the fire escape tonight to try to find it.

"It's easy to find Sirius," Ms. Thomas was saying, "because it's the brightest star we can see." She rolled to a sitting position and squeezed Ruth's shoulder. "Sometimes, it even casts a shadow."

The whole rest of the day Ruth found it hard

to concentrate. She kept looking out the window at the cars below, and the people walking their dogs, and the ladies pushing strollers. She pictured a world bigger than the classroom, bigger than Manhattan, bigger than the boundaries of her imagination.

The scariest part of the Presidential Physical Fitness Test was climbing the rope that hung from the ceiling of the tiny gymnasium. There were two: one with knots, and one without. Ruth was worried she couldn't even shimmy her way up the one with knots. You had to excel at all the sections: the shuttle run, the one-mile run, the curl-ups, the pull-ups, the rope climb, the V-sit reach. If you did, you got a gold certificate as an award.

Ruth, who got straight As, didn't like failing at anything, even gym class.

Because of their last names, it was Maia's turn just before Ruth's. She picked the rope with the knots (girls had a choice, boys didn't) and made it halfway up before she started to panic.

Her eyes squirreled shut and her face went red and she clutched the rope like it was a lifeline. Even when Mr. Yorkey, the gym teacher, told her to come on down, she couldn't unhook herself. It took two other teachers to help pry her off the rope, and when Maia reached ground level the other girls flocked around her like worker bees to the queen. Lola was chosen to help walk Maia to the nurse's office.

When it was Ruth's turn, she wiped her hands on her shorts and pulled with all her might to anchor her feet to the bottom knot. Then she closed her eyes and inched her right hand up to the next highest knot, and then her left, and then she crunched her legs up until her feet found their next hold. She did this again, picturing herself as a caterpillar, bunching and relaxing, concentrating only on getting to a knot higher than the one Maia had reached. When her hand reached up to grab the next knot and instead she found the bell on the ceiling to ring, signaling that she'd reached the top, she was surprised. She skittered down the rope, flushed and proud, and imagined coming home with that gold certificate. Mama would put it up on the refrigerator.

About fifteen minutes later Maia walked back into the gymnasium, this time accompanied by the school nurse. Ruth heard the nurse say words like *panic attack* and *heights* and *sue,* and Mr. Yorkey agreed to let Maia sit out the rest of the test, and to be his assistant instead. He showed her how to work the stopwatch, and she sat on the start line of the mile run (eight laps around the gym track).

"Seamus, you're up," Mr. Yorkey said. "Ruth, on deck."

Ruth stood awkwardly next to Maia, not sure if she should say something like *I hope you're feeling better now*. But she didn't know how without it coming out sounding like Ruth was lording over her the fact that she had rung the bell and Maia hadn't, and pride was a sin, so instead, she just tugged at the bottom of her shorts and scuffed her sneaker on the squeaky polyurethaned floor. It sounded like a chipmunk.

Maia pushed the button on the stopwatch to get it ready. Ruth put her toe on the red starting line, as close to the inside edge as she could, without cheating.

"On your mark," Mr. Yorkey called out.

"Hey, Ruth?" Maia said quietly.

"Get set . . ."

Ruth twisted her neck.

"You're gonna ace this," Maia said, smiling. "Just run like the KKK is chasing you."

"Go!" Mr. Yorkey shouted.

Last year Granny's best friend in the world had died of cancer. She and Miz Lonnie had come up north from Mississippi when they were seventeen and had gotten jobs in a factory together and got married a year apart. Miz Lonnie was the sister she'd never had, and at her funeral, Granny wept so hard that she had to be helped out of the church.

She took to her bed, drinking the medicinal whiskey. An hour later Ruth cracked the door open to make sure she was all right, because it was scary to see someone you were used to envisioning as the very definition of solid break into pieces before your eyes. Granny was sitting on the bed, still in her black lace dress, a shoe box in her lap. Spread all around her were photographs so old that they had wavy edges, with handwritten ink on the back that had turned brown with age. "Baby girl, you come sit with me," Granny said, and Ruth crawled onto the mattress and tucked herself tight underneath the old woman's arm.

Ruth pointed to one scalloped photo. "Is that you, Granny?"

The picture was of a woman younger than Mama, even, with hair pulled back into a bun and a crisp white shirt tucked into her skirt. She was pointing at the camera and laughing.

"That's me," Granny said. "And look, in the background here, that's your great-granny." Ruth looked closer and saw a woman with a pinched mouth standing on the porch in the background, her arms crossed. "She was mad because Lonnie and me, we were always foolin' around."

"Where's Miz Lonnie?" Ruth asked.

"On the other side of the camera," Granny explained. "She had just got it that day, and she said I could be her model."

Ruth snuggled closer. Granny smelled of talcum powder and rosewater and Maker's Mark. "What about this one?" she said, holding up a picture of four austere youths—two young men stiffly holding the elbows of Granny and Miz Lonnie, who wore flower corsages that had been bleached white by the exposure process.

"Well, that was a church social. Lonnie, she was wild for that boy, but she wasn't allowed to go on her own, so he brought along a friend as my date. Go figure, I fell hard for him."

"That's Granddaddy?" Ruth asked.

"No, his name was Jerald. He was the first boy I loved. Granddaddy was the last."

They sat on the bed sifting through the entire shoe box, each photograph a memory. Granny talked about creeks she used to swim in with Miz Lonnie and the coonhound her family had that used to attack porcupines. She pointed to a gold cross Ruth's great-granny wore in one picture, which was the same gold cross Granny had around her neck at that very moment. There was a photo of her and Miz Lonnie in Times Square with old-time cars that Ruth had seen only in movies, and one of Granny pregnant with Mama, holding Miz Lonnie's toddler son, Abraham, like he was a practice run. Then Ruth found a picture that had gotten wedged in the cardboard at the side. This one, though, wasn't from Miz Lonnie's camera. It was a newspaper clipping of a hanged man. "What happened to him?" Ruth asked.

"The KKK happened to him," Granny said. She reached for her bottle of whiskey and took another shot. "White men, with their pointy hoods, burning their crosses." She breathed fire at Ruth, who closed her eyes and held her nose. "They killed him. Lonnie and me, we saw it on the way to school. And I near passed out, but Lonnie, she caught me and she told me we had to get away. We were gonna leave town and go somewhere things like this never happened—"

Just then, Mama came into the bedroom. "What on earth is going on here?" she demanded, as Ruth slipped the newspaper clipping under her leg. Mama sniffed the air and frowned, taking the whiskey bottle and the shot glass off Granny's nightstand. "What kind of example you setting?" she chided, and to Ruth she said, "That's enough. You leave Granny to get some rest." As Ruth curled the newspaper clipping into her hand, Mama pulled back the covers and took off Granny's shoes, helping her get to bed. "Why you telling Ruth about all that?" Mama said. "She's a baby!"

By now Granny was slurring her words. "Them crackas wasn't shit," she muttered. "We left town and didn't look back. We left before Jerald even got buried."

Ruth hid the newspaper clipping underneath her mattress. Sometimes she would take it out and look at it, but the image was grainy and she couldn't connect that poor man with the one in a suit and tie who had stood for a formal photo holding Granny's arm like it was made of fine china. She couldn't imagine the man twisting on that rope picking out carnations and baby's breath for a pretty corsage.

Sometimes at night, Ruth would wonder: If not for the KKK, would Granny have stayed in Mississippi and married Jerald? If not for the KKK, would Ruth even be here?

"Go!" Mr. Yorkey shouted, and Ruth did.

She pivoted on her foot, and instead of running the mile to get a gold certificate of presidential fitness, she threw herself at Maia, yanking at her glossy ponytail, rolling with her on the floor until Ruth had her pinned down, one forearm across Maia's collarbones while the other hand drew back in a fist.

"Go ahead," Maia dared. "Punch me."

Ruth was so surprised, she hesitated.

"Because then you'll just wind up cleaning toilets like your mother."

Ruth could feel her heart beating so hard, it was practically external. She was sweating, her hair coming out of its elastic to curl natural around her face. It was like Cinderella all over again, turning back into her rags with her pumpkin.

She let go of Maia abruptly and walked away from her, her back to the rest of the class, which had gone absolutely silent watching the show.

Mr. Yorkey grasped her arm firmly. "Ruth," he said, "would you like to go sit down and control your emotions?"

She faced the gym teacher. "No," Ruth said honestly, because what she really wanted to do was smack Maia. What she really wanted to do was go back in time ten minutes to the moment before Maia had said anything. Or maybe further—say, two months—before she had ever set foot in this school.

"Go to the program director's office," Mr. Yorkey said tightly. "Now."

The director of First Program at Dalton was a very thin woman named Mrs. Grau-Lerner, who smelled of mothballs and peppermint. Ruth, who had never been sent to the principal's office in her life, was shivering.

"Do you know what you did wrong, Ruth?" Mrs. Grau-Lerner asked.

Ruth shook her head. She hadn't hit Maia, although she had wanted to, so why was she being punished?

"Not only were you involved in an altercation . . . you also were rude to Mr. Yorkey."

Ruth looked up at her. She thought Mr. Yorkey had been asking her a question. She didn't realize it was actually a test.

If Mr. Yorkey had wanted her to sit down and cool off, he should have told her so. Had it been Mama, for example, she would have said, *Do your homework*. No wiggle room there, just a direct order. Instead, Mr. Yorkey had given Ruth a choice, and now she was being disciplined for taking it.

"Mrs. Grau-Lerner, Maia said—"

The woman held up her hand. "Ruth," she replied, "we don't blame others at Dalton. We take responsibility for our own actions."

Ruth looked into her lap. "Yes, ma'am," she said.

Suddenly there was a knock on the director's office door, and a secretary opened it. "Ms. Brooks is here," she said, and through the slice that was opened Ruth could see Mama still in her uniform, crackling with questions.

"Why don't you wait in Ms. Thomas's room while I speak with your mother?" Mrs. Grau-Lerner said.

Ruth slipped out of the office and past her mama with her eyes cast down. She knew there would be a reckoning in private. She walked to the classroom, which was empty because all the other students in Ms. Thomas's class were still getting tested in the gymnasium. She sat down at her desk, and then stood up and walked toward the front of the classroom.

She picked up the chalk and wrote her name on the board, underneath that night's homework assignment. Then she erased it, so that you couldn't see the letters. Just a ghost that let you know something had been there.

* * *

Mama was mad, all right, but not at Ruth. "Social difficulties, my foot," she muttered under her breath, as they boarded the bus together. "More like they're the ones who are having trouble adjusting. Can't deal with the *climate,* what does that even mean?"

Ruth was afraid to speak. If she did, then she would have to tell Mama about Maia and what she'd said, and she didn't want to do that. But the bus stopped at the spot where they should have gotten off to go to Ms. Mina's, and they stayed on. It wasn't following the uptown route to Harlem. Ruth had no idea where they were headed.

Maybe Mama was so angry she had forgotten to get off the bus.

"Mama," Ruth asked in a small voice. "Where we going?"

In response, Mama pushed the cord for the next stop and took Ruth's hand. They got off the bus, belched into the frenetic hurry of 42nd Street. Ruth huddled closer to Mama, avoiding tourists who were pointing at the lighted billboards and the girls in too little clothes and too much makeup who checked their reflections in the windows of fancy restaurants.

"Here we go," Mama announced, walking into a small store that sold gloves and barrettes and scarves and any other accessory you could think of. Maybe Ms. Mina had been sending Mama on an errand when she got diverted to the school. Ruth trailed her fingers along a display of hanging earrings that were made of feathers and tiny woven dream catchers.

"Ruth," Mama called, and she turned around. "Is this what you were talking about?"

She was pointing to a case of glittering rhinestone headbands, each brighter than the next. On their blue velvet field, they looked like constellations.

Sirius, Ruth thought.

"Pick one," Mama said.

Ruth blinked, shocked. Of all the outcomes she could have imagined, being rewarded for getting sent to the program director's office was not one of them. "Mama," she said, "I don't need it . . ."

"Oh yes you do," she said. She pointed to one that looked like a string of daisies, made of crystals. "That's pretty."

Ruth nodded.

"You know how I wear a uniform? It's so Ms. Mina and Mr. Sam and everyone else in that building recognizes who I am. This is *your* uniform." Her mama picked up the daisy band and settled it gently on Ruth's head, like she was being crowned. "If this is what it takes to make them see you," she said, "then so be it."

Although Ruth knew she wasn't allowed out on the fire escape because Mama thought it was unsafe, she waited until everyone was asleep and then crawled outside. She lay on her back, careful not to get too close to the edge, and stared up at the stars. It was easy to find Sirius, as Ms. Thomas had said. It was by far the brightest, shining even through the smog and the clouds and the ambient light of the city.

Ruth reached up and touched her rhinestone headband. She thought about the bright beam that had left Sirius eight and a half years ago. It was reaching her fire escape and Christina's home and Dalton all at once. No matter where you stood, you'd be underneath the same light.

Follow Ruth's unforgettable story in Jodi Picoult's eye-opening new novel, *Small Great Things*, available now.

Read on for an extract . . .

Ruth

The miracle happened on West 74th Street, in the home where Mama worked. It was a big brownstone encircled by a wrought-iron fence, and overlooking either side of the ornate door were gargoyles, their granite faces carved from my nightmares. They terrified me, so I didn't mind the fact that we always entered through the less-impressive side door, whose keys Mama kept on a ribbon in her purse.

Mama had been working for Sam Hallowell and his family since before my sister and I were born. You may not have recognized his name, but you would have known him the minute he said hello. He had been the unmistakable voice in the mid-1960s who announced before every show: *The following program is brought to you in living color on NBC!* In 1976, when the miracle happened, he was the network's head of programming. The doorbell beneath those gargoyles was the famously pitched three-note chime everyone associates with NBC. Sometimes, when I came to work with my mother, I'd sneak outside and push the button and hum along.

The reason we were with Mama that day was because it was a snow day. School was canceled, but we were too little to stay alone in our apartment while Mama went to work – which she did, through snow and sleet and probably also earthquakes and Armageddon. She muttered, stuffing us into our snowsuits and boots, that it didn't matter if she had to cross a blizzard to do it, but God forbid Ms Mina had to spread the peanut butter on her own sandwich bread. In fact the only time I remember Mama taking time off work was twenty-five years later, when she had a double hip replacement, generously paid for by the Hallowells. She stayed home for a week, and even after that, when it didn't quite heal right and she insisted on returning to work, Mina found her tasks to do that kept her off her feet. But when I was little, during school vacations and bouts of fever and snow days like this one, Mama would take us with her on the B train downtown.

Mr Hallowell was away in California that week, which happened often, and which meant that Ms Mina and Christina needed Mama even more. So did Rachel and I, but we were better at taking care of ourselves, I suppose, than Ms Mina was.

When we finally emerged at 72nd Street, the world was white. It was not just that Central Park was caught in a snow globe. The faces of the men and women shuddering through the storm to get to work looked nothing like mine, or like my cousins' or neighbors'.

I had not been into any Manhattan homes except for the Hallowells', so I didn't know how extraordinary it was for one family to live, alone, in this huge building. But I remember thinking it made no sense that Rachel and I had to put our snowsuits and boots into the tiny, cramped closet in the kitchen, when there were plenty of empty hooks and open spaces in the main entry, where Christina's and Ms Mina's coats were hanging. Mama tucked away her coat, too, and her lucky scarf – the soft one that smelled like her, and that Rachel and I fought to wear around our house because it felt like petting a guinea pig or a bunny under your fingers. I waited for Mama to move through the dark rooms like Tinker Bell, alighting on a switch or a handle or a knob so that the sleeping beast of a house was gradually brought to life.

'You two be quiet,' Mama told us, 'and I'll make you some of Ms Mina's hot chocolate.'

It was imported from Paris, and it tasted like heaven. So as Mama tied on her white apron, I took a piece of paper from a kitchen drawer and a packet of crayons I'd brought from home and silently started to sketch. I made a house as big as this one. I put a family inside: me, Mama, Rachel. I tried to draw snow, but I couldn't. The flakes I'd made with the white crayon were invisible on the paper. The only way to see them was to tilt the paper sideways toward the chandelier light, so I could make out the shimmer where the crayon had been.

'Can we play with Christina?' Rachel asked. Christina was six, falling neatly between the ages of Rachel and me. Christina had the biggest bedroom I had ever seen and more toys than anyone I knew. When she was home and we came to work with our mother, we played school with her and her teddy bears, drank water out of real miniature china teacups, and braided the corn-silk hair of her dolls. Unless she had a friend over, in which case we stayed in the kitchen and colored.

But before Mama could answer, there was a scream so piercing and so ragged that it stabbed me in the chest. I knew it did the same to Mama, because she nearly dropped the pot of water she was carrying to the sink. 'Stay here,' she said, her voice already trailing behind her as she ran upstairs.

Rachel was the first one out of her chair; she

wasn't one to follow instructions. I was drawn in her wake, a balloon tied to her wrist. My hand skimmed over the banister of the curved staircase, not touching.

Ms Mina's bedroom door was wide open, and she was twisting on the bed in a sinkhole of satin sheets. The round of her belly rose like a moon; the shining whites of her eyes made me think of merry-go-round horses, frozen in flight. 'It's too early, Lou,' she gasped.

'Tell that to this baby,' Mama replied. She was holding the telephone receiver. Ms Mina held her other hand in a death grip. 'You stop pushing, now,' she said. 'The ambulance'll be here any minute.'

I wondered how fast an ambulance could get here in all that snow.

'Mommy?'

It wasn't until I heard Christina's voice that I realized the noise had woken her up. She stood between Rachel and me. 'You three, go to Miss Christina's room,' Mama ordered, with steel in her voice. '*Now*.'

But we remained rooted to the spot as Mama quickly forgot about us, lost in a world made of Ms Mina's pain and fear, trying to be the map that she could follow out of it. I watched the cords stand out on Ms Mina's neck as she groaned; I saw Mama kneel on the bed between her legs and push her gown over her knees. I watched the pink lips between Ms Mina's legs purse and swell and part. There was the round knob of a head, a knot of shoulder, a gush of blood and fluid, and suddenly, a baby was cradled in Mama's palms.

'Look at you,' she said, with love written over her face. 'Weren't you in a hurry to get into this world?'

Two things happened at once: the doorbell rang, and Christina started to cry. 'Oh, honey,' Ms Mina crooned, not scary anymore but still sweaty and red-faced. She held out her hand, but Christina was too terrified by what she had seen, and instead she burrowed closer to me. Rachel, ever practical, went to answer the front door. She returned with two paramedics, who swooped in and took over, so that what Mama had done for Ms Mina became like everything else she did for the Hallowells: seamless and invisible.

The Hallowells named the baby Louis, after Mama. He was fine, even though he was almost a full month early, a casualty of the barometric pressure dropping with the storm, which caused a PROM – a premature rupture of membranes. Of course, I didn't know that back then. I only knew that on a snowy day in Manhattan I had seen the very start of someone. I'd been with that baby before anyone or anything in this world had a chance to disappoint him.

The experience of watching Louis being born affected us all differently. Christina had her baby via surrogate. Rachel had five. Me, I became a labor and delivery nurse.

When I tell people this story, they assume the miracle I am referring to during that long-ago blizzard was the birth of a baby. True, that was astonishing. But that day I witnessed a greater wonder. As Christina held my hand and Ms

Mina held Mama's, there was a moment – one heartbeat, one breath – where all the differences in schooling and money and skin color evaporated like mirages in a desert. Where everyone was equal, and it was just one woman, helping another.

That miracle, I've spent thirty-nine years waiting to see again.

Stage One

Active Labor

Not everything that is faced can be changed.
But nothing can be changed until it is faced.

                              – JAMES BALDWIN

Ruth

The most beautiful baby I ever saw was born without a face.

From the neck down, he was perfect: ten fingers, ten toes, chubby belly. But where his ear should have been, there was a twist of lips and a single tooth. Instead of a face there was a swirling eddy of skin with no features.

His mother – my patient – was a thirty-year-old gravida 1 para 1 who had received prenatal care including an ultrasound, but the baby had been positioned in a way that the facial deformity hadn't been visible. The spine, the heart, the organs had all looked fine, so no one was expecting this. Maybe for that very reason, she chose to deliver at Mercy–West Haven, our little cottage hospital, and not Yale–New Haven, which is better equipped for emergencies. She came in full term, and labored for sixteen hours before she delivered. The doctor lifted the baby, and there was nothing but silence. Buzzy, white silence.

'Is he all right?' the mother asked, panicking. 'Why isn't he crying?'

I had a student nurse shadowing me, and she screamed.

'Get out,' I said tightly, shoving her from the room. Then I took the newborn from the obstetrician and placed him on the warmer, wiping the vernix from his limbs. The OB did a quick exam, silently met my gaze, and turned back to the parents, who by now knew something was terribly wrong. In soft words, the doctor said their child had profound birth defects that were incompatible with life.

On a birth pavilion, Death is a more common patient than you'd think. When we have anencephalies or fetal deaths, we know that the parents still have to bond with and mourn for that baby. This infant – alive, for however long that might be – was still this couple's son.

So I cleaned him and swaddled him, the way I would any other newborn, while the conversation behind me between the parents and the doctor stopped and started like a car choking through the winter. *Why? How? What if you . . .? How long until . . .?* Questions no one ever wants to ask, and no one ever wants to answer.

The mother was still crying when I settled the baby in the crook of her elbow. His tiny hands windmilled. She smiled down at him, her heart in her eyes. 'Ian,' she whispered. 'Ian Michael Barnes.'

She wore an expression I've only seen in paintings in museums, of a love and a grief so fierce that they forged together to create some new, raw emotion.

I turned to the father. 'Would you like to hold your son?'

He looked like he was about to be sick. 'I can't,' he muttered and bolted from the room.

I followed him, but was intercepted by the

nurse in training, who was apologetic and upset. 'I'm sorry,' she said. 'It's just . . . it was a *monster*.'

'It *is* a *baby*,' I corrected, and I pushed past her.

I cornered the father in the parents' lounge. 'Your wife and your son need you.'

'That's not my son,' he said. 'That . . . thing . . .'

'Is not going to be on this earth for very long. Which means you'd better give him all the love you had stored up for his lifetime right now.' I waited until he looked me in the eye, and then I turned on my heel. I did not have to glance back to know he was following me.

When we entered the hospital room, his wife was still nuzzling the infant, her lips pressed to the smooth canvas of his brow. I took the tiny bundle from her arms, and handed the baby to her husband. He sucked in his breath and then drew back the blanket from the spot where the baby's face should have been.

I've thought about my actions, you know. If I did the right thing by forcing the father to confront his dying baby, if it was my place as a nurse. Had my supervisor asked me at the time, I would have said that I'd been trained to provide closure for grieving parents. If this man didn't acknowledge that something truly horrible had happened – or worse, if he kept pretending for the rest of his life that it never *had* – a hole would open up inside him. Tiny at first, that pit would wear away, bigger and bigger, until one day when he wasn't expecting it he would realize he was completely hollow.

When the father started to cry, the sobs shook his body, like a hurricane bends a tree. He sank down beside his wife on the hospital bed, and she put one hand on her husband's back and one on the crown of the baby's head.

They took turns holding their son for ten hours. That mother, she even tried to let him nurse. I could not stop staring – not because it was ugly or wrong, but because it was the most remarkable thing I'd ever seen. It felt like looking into the face of the sun: once I turned away, I was blind to everything else.

At one point, I took that stupid nursing

student into the room with me, ostensibly to check the mother's vitals, but really to make her see with her own eyes how love has nothing to do with what you're looking at, and everything to do with who's looking.

When the infant died, it was peaceful. We made casts of the newborn's hand and foot for the parents to keep. I heard that this same couple came back two years later and delivered a healthy daughter, though I wasn't on duty when it happened.

It just goes to show you: every baby is born beautiful.

It's what we project on them that makes them ugly.

*

Right after I gave birth to Edison, seventeen years ago at this very hospital, I wasn't worried about the health of my baby, or how I was going to juggle being a single parent while my husband was overseas, or how my life was going to change now that I was a mother.

I was worried about my hair.

The last thing you're thinking about when you're in labor is what you look like, but if you're like me, it's the first thing that crosses your mind once that baby's come. The sweat that mats the hair of all my white patients to their foreheads instead made my roots curl up and pull away from the scalp. Brushing my hair around my head in a swirl like an ice cream cone and wrapping it in a scarf each night was what kept it straight the next day when I took it down. But what white nurse knew that, or understood that the little complimentary bottle of shampoo provided by the hospital auxiliary league was only going to make my hair even frizzier? I was sure that when my well-meaning colleagues came in to meet Edison, they would be shocked into stupor at the sight of the mess going on atop my head.

In the end, I wound up wrapping it in a towel, and told visitors I'd just had a shower.

I know nurses who work on surgical floors who tell me about men wheeled out of surgery who insist on taping their toupees into place in the recovery room before their spouses join them. And I can't tell you the number of times a patient who has spent the night grunting and screaming and pushing out a baby with her husband at her side will kick her spouse out of the room postdelivery so I can help her put on a pretty nightgown and robe.

I understand the need people have to put a certain face on for the rest of the world. Which is why – when I first arrive for my shift at 6:40 A.M. – I don't even go into the staff room, where we will shortly receive the night's update from the charge nurse. Instead I slip down the hall to the patient I'd been with yesterday, before my shift ended. Her name was Jessie; she was a tiny little thing who had come into the pavilion looking more like a campaigning First Lady than a woman in active labor: her hair was perfectly coiffed, her face airbrushed with makeup, even her maternity clothes were fitted and stylish. That's a dead giveaway, since by forty weeks of pregnancy most mothers-to-be would be happy to wear a pup tent. I scanned her chart – G1, now P1 – and grinned. The last thing I'd said to Jessie before I turned her care over to a colleague and went home for the night was that the next time I saw her, she'd have a baby, and sure enough, I have a new patient. While I've been sleeping, Jessie's delivered a healthy seven-pound, six-ounce girl.

I open the door to find Jessie dozing. The baby lies swaddled in the bassinet beside the bed; Jessie's husband is sprawled in a chair, snoring. Jessie stirs when I walk in, and I immediately put a finger to my lips. *Quiet*.

From my purse, I pull a compact mirror and a red lipstick.

Part of labor is conversation; it's the distraction that makes the pain ebb and it's the glue that bonds a nurse to her patient. What other situation can you think of where one medical professional spends up to twelve hours consulting with a single person? As a result, the connection we build with these women is fierce and fast. I know things about them, in a mere matter of hours, that their own closest friends don't always know: how she met her partner at a bar when she'd had too much to drink; how her father didn't live long enough to see this grandchild; how she worries about being a mom because she hated babysitting as a teenager. Last night, in the dragon hours of Jessie's labor, when she was teary and exhausted and snapping at her husband, I'd suggested that he go to the cafeteria to get a cup of coffee. As soon as he left, the air in the room was easier to breathe, and she fell back against those awful plastic pillows we have in the birthing pavilion. 'What if this baby changes everything?' she sobbed. She confessed that she never went anywhere without her 'game face' on, that her husband had never even seen her without mascara; and now here he was watching her body contort itself inside out, and how would he ever look at her the same way again?

Listen, I had told her. *You let* me *worry about that.*

I'd like to think my taking that one straw

off her back was what gave her the strength to make it to transition.

It's funny. When I tell people I've been a labor and delivery nurse for more than twenty years, they're impressed by the fact that I have assisted in cesareans, that I can start an IV in my sleep, that I can tell the difference between a decel in the fetal heart rate that is normal and one that requires intervention. But for me, being an L & D nurse is all about knowing your patient, and what she needs. A back rub. An epidural. A little Maybelline.

Jessie glances at her husband, still dead to the world. Then she takes the lipstick from my hand. 'Thank you,' she whispers, and our eyes connect. I hold the mirror as she once again re-invents herself.

On Thursdays, my shift goes from 7:00 A.M. till 7:00 P.M. At Mercy–West Haven, during the day, we usually have two nurses on the birthing pavilion – three if we're swimming in human resources that day. As I walk through the pavilion, I note idly how many of our delivery suites are occupied – it's three, right now, a nice slow start to the day. Marie, the charge nurse, is already in the room where we have our morning meeting when I come inside, but Corinne – the second nurse on shift with me – is missing. 'What's it going to be today?' Marie asks, as she flips through the morning paper.

'Flat tire,' I reply. This guessing game is a routine: *What excuse will Corinne use today for being late?* It's a beautiful fall day in October, so she can't blame the weather.

'That was last week. I'm going with the flu.'

'Speaking of which,' I say. 'How's Ella?' Marie's eight-year-old had caught the stomach bug that's been going around.

'Back in school today, thank God,' Marie replies. 'Now Dave's got it. I figure I have twenty-four hours before I'm down for the count.' She looks up from the Regional section of the paper. 'I saw Edison's name in here again,' she says.

My son has made the Highest Honors list for every semester of his high school career. But just like I tell him, that's no reason to boast. 'There are a lot of bright kids in this town,' I demur.

'Still,' Marie says. 'For a boy like Edison to be so successful . . . well. You should be proud, is all. I can only hope Ella turns out to be that good a student.'

A boy like Edison. I know what she is saying, even if she's careful not to spell it out. There are not many Black kids in the high school, and as far as I know, Edison is the only one on the Highest Honors list. Comments like this feel like paper cuts, but I've worked with Marie for over ten years now, so I try to ignore the sting. I know she doesn't really mean anything by it. She's a friend, after all – she came to my house with her family for Easter supper last year, along with some of the other nurses, and we've gone out for cocktails or movie nights and once a girls' weekend at a spa. Still, Marie has no idea how often I have to just take a deep breath, and move on. White people don't mean half the offensive things that come out of their mouths, and so I try not to let myself get rubbed the wrong way.

'Maybe you should hope that Ella makes it through the school day without going to the nurse's office again,' I reply, and Marie laughs.

'You're right. First things first.'

Corinne explodes into the room. 'Sorry I'm late,' she says, and Marie and I exchange a look. Corinne's fifteen years younger than I am, and there's always some emergency – a carburetor that's dead, a fight with her boyfriend, a crash on 95N. Corinne is one of those people for whom life is just the space between crises. She takes off her coat and manages to knock over a potted plant that died months ago, which no one has bothered to replace. 'Dammit,' she mutters, righting the pot and sweeping the soil back inside. She dusts off her palms on her scrubs, and then sits down with her hands folded. 'I'm really sorry, Marie. The stupid tire I replaced last week has a leak or something; I had to drive here the whole way going thirty.'

Marie reaches into her pocket and pulls out a dollar, which she flicks across the table at me. I laugh.

'All right,' Marie says. 'Floor report. Room two is a couplet. Jessica Myers, G one P one at forty weeks and two days. She had a vaginal delivery this morning at three A.M., uncomplicated, without pain meds. Baby girl is breast-feeding well; she's peed but hasn't pooped yet.'

'I'll take her,' Corinne and I say in unison.

Everyone wants the patient who's already delivered; it's the easier job. 'I had her during active labor,' I point out.

'Right,' Marie says. 'Ruth, she's yours.' She pushes her reading glasses up on her nose. 'Room three is Thea McVaughn, G one P zero at forty-one weeks and three days, she's in active labor at four centimeters dilated, membranes intact. Fetal heart rate tracing looks good on the monitor, the baby's active. She's requested an epidural and her IV fluid bolus is infusing.'

'Has Anesthesia been paged?' Corinne asks.

'Yes.'

'I've got her.'

We only take one active labor patient at a time, if we can help it, which means that the third patient – the last one this morning – will be mine. 'Room five is a recovery. Brittany Bauer is a G one P one at thirty-nine weeks and one day; had an epidural and a vaginal delivery at five-thirty A.M. Baby's a boy; they want a circ. Mom was a GDM A one; the baby is on Q three hour blood sugars for twenty-four hours. The mom really wants to breast-feed. They're still skin to skin.'

A recovery is still a lot of work – a one-to-one nurse-patient relationship. True, the labor's finished, but there is still tidying up to be done, a physical assessment of the newborn, and a stack of paperwork. 'Got it,' I say, and I push away from the table to go find Lucille, the night nurse, who was with Brittany during the delivery.

She finds me first, in the staff restroom, washing my hands. 'Tag, you're it,' she says, handing me Brittany Bauer's file. 'Twenty-six-year-old G one, now P one, delivered vaginally this morning at five-thirty over an intact perineum. She's O positive, rubella immune, Hep

B and HIV negative, GBS negative. Gestational diabetic, diet controlled, otherwise uncomplicated. She still has an IV in her left forearm. I DC'd the epidural, but she hasn't been out of bed yet, so ask her if she has to get up and pee. Her bleeding's been good, her fundus is firm at U.'

I open the file and scan the notes, committing the details to memory. 'Davis,' I read. 'That's the baby?'

'Yeah. His vital signs have been normal, but his one-hour blood sugar was forty, so we've got him trying to nurse. He's done a little bit on each side, but he's kind of spitty and sleepy and he hasn't done a whole lot of eating.'

'Did he get his eyes and thighs?'

'Yeah, and he's peed, but hasn't pooped. I haven't done the bath or the newborn assessment yet.'

'No problem,' I say. 'Is that it?'

'The dad's name is Turk,' Lucille replies, hesitating. 'There's something just a little . . . off about him.'

'Like Creeper Dad?' I ask. Last year, we had a father who was flirting with the nursing student in the room during his wife's delivery. When she wound up having a C-section, instead of standing behind the drape near his wife's head, he strolled across the OR and said to the nursing student, *Is it hot in here, or is it just you?*

'Not like that,' Lucille says. 'He's appropriate with the mom. He's just . . . sketchy. I can't put my finger on it.'

I've always thought that if I wasn't an L & D nurse, I'd make a great fake psychic. We are skilled at reading our patients so that we know what they need moments before they realize it. And we are also gifted when it comes to sensing strange vibes. Just last month my radar went off when a mentally challenged patient came in with an older Ukrainian woman who had befriended her at the grocery store where she worked. There was something weird about the dynamic between them, and I followed my hunch and called the police. Turned out the Ukrainian woman had served time in Kentucky for stealing the baby of a woman with Down syndrome.

So as I walk into Brittany Bauer's room for the first time, I am not worried. I'm thinking: *I've got this.*

I knock softly and push open the door. 'I'm Ruth,' I say. 'I'm going to be your nurse today.' I walk right up to Brittany, and smile down at the baby cradled in her arms. 'Isn't he a sweetie! What's his name?' I ask, although I already know. It's a means to start a conversation, to connect with the patient.

Brittany doesn't answer. She looks at her husband, a hulking guy who's sitting on the edge of his chair. He's got military-short hair and he's bouncing the heel of one boot like he can't quite stay still. I get what Lucille saw in him. Turk Bauer makes me think of a power line that's snapped during a storm, and lies across the road just waiting for something to brush against it so it can shoot sparks.

It doesn't matter if you're shy or modest – nobody who's just had a baby stays quiet for long. They *want* to share this life-changing moment. They *want* to relive the labor, the birth, the beauty of their baby. But Brittany, well, it's almost like she needs his permission to speak. *Domestic abuse?* I wonder.

'Davis,' she chokes out. 'His name is Davis.'

'Well, hello, Davis,' I murmur, moving closer to the bed. 'Would you mind if I take a listen to his heart and lungs and check his temperature?'

Her arms clamp tighter on the newborn, pulling him closer.

'I can do it right here,' I say. 'You don't have to let go of him.'

You have to cut a new parent a little bit of slack, especially one who's already been told her baby's blood sugar is too low. So I tuck the thermometer under Davis's armpit, and get a normal reading. I look at the whorls of his hair – a patch of white can signify hearing loss; an alternating hair pattern can flag metabolic issues. I press my stethoscope against the baby's back, listening to his lungs. I slide my hand between him and his mother, listening to his heart.

Whoosh.

It's so faint that I think it's a mistake.

I listen again, trying to make sure it wasn't a fluke, but that slight whir is there behind the backbeat of the pulse.

Turk stands up so that he is towering over me; he folds his arms.

Nerves look different on fathers. They get combative, sometimes. As if they could bluster away whatever's wrong.

'I hear a very slight murmur,' I say delicately. 'But it could be nothing. This early, there are still parts of the heart that are developing. Even if it *is* a murmur, it could disappear in a few days. Still, I'll make a note of it; I'll have the pediatrician take a listen.' While I'm talking, trying to be as calm as possible, I do another blood sugar. It's an Accu-Chek, which means we get instant results – and this time, he's at fifty-two. 'Now, *this* is great news,' I say, trying to give the Bauers something positive to hold on to. 'His sugar is much better.' I walk to the sink and run warm water, fill a plastic bowl, and set it on the warmer. 'Davis is definitely perking up, and he'll probably start eating really soon. Why don't I get him cleaned up, and fire him up a little bit, and we can try nursing again?'

I reach down and scoop the baby up. Turning my back to the parents, I place Davis on the warmer and begin my exam. I can hear Brittany and Turk whispering fiercely as I check the fontanels on the baby's head for the suture lines, to make sure the bones aren't overriding each other. The parents are worried, and that's normal. A lot of patients don't like to take the nurse's opinion on any medical issue; they need to hear it from the doctor to believe it – even though L & D nurses are often the ones who first notice a quirk or a symptom. Their pediatrician is Atkins; I will page her after I'm done with the exam, and have her listen to the baby's heart.

But right now, my attention is on Davis. I look for facial bruising, hematoma, or abnormal shaping of the skull. I check the palmar creases in his tiny hands, and the set of his ears relative to his eyes. I measure the circumference of his head and the length of his squirming body. I check for clefts in the mouth and the ears. I palpate the clavicles and put my pinkie in his mouth to check his sucking reflex. I study the rise and fall of the tiny bellows of his chest, to make sure his breathing isn't labored. Press his belly to make sure it's soft, check his fingers and toes, scan for rashes or lesions or birthmarks. I make sure his testicles have descended and scan for hypospadias, making sure that the urethra is where it's supposed to be. Then I gently turn him over and scan the base of the spine for dimples or hair tufts or any other indicator of neural tube defect.

I realize that the whispering behind me has stopped. But instead of feeling more comfortable, it feels ominous. *What do they think I'm doing wrong?*

By the time I flip him back over, Davis's eyes are starting to drift shut. Babies usually get sleepy a couple of hours after delivery, which is one reason to do the bath now – it will wake him up long enough to try to feed again. There is a stack of wipes on the warmer; with practiced, sure strokes I dip one into the warm water and wipe the baby down from head to toe. Then I diaper him, swiftly wrap him up in a blanket like a burrito, and rinse his hair under the sink with some Johnson's baby shampoo. The last thing I do is put an ID band on him that will match the ones his parents have, and fasten a tiny electronic security bracelet on his ankle, which will set off an alarm if the baby gets too close to any of the exits.

I can feel the parents' eyes, hot on my back. I turn, a smile fastened on my face. 'There,' I say, handing the infant to Brittany again. 'Clean as a whistle. Now, let's see if we can get him to nurse.'

I reach down to help position the baby, but Brittany flinches.

'Get away from her,' Turk Bauer says. 'I want to talk to your boss.'

They are the first words he has spoken to me in the twenty minutes I've been in this room with him and his family, and they carry an undercurrent of discontent. I'm pretty sure he doesn't want to tell Marie what a stellar job I've done. But I nod tightly and step out of the room, replaying every word and gesture I have made since introducing myself to Brittany Bauer. I walk to the nurses' desk and find Marie filling out a chart. 'We've got a problem in Five,' I say, trying to keep my voice even. 'The father wants to see you.'

'What happened?' Marie asks.

'Absolutely nothing,' I reply, and I know it's true. I'm a good nurse. Sometimes a great one. I took care of that infant the way I would have taken care of any newborn on this pavilion. 'I told them I heard what sounded like a murmur, and that I'd contact the pediatrician. And I bathed the baby and did his exam.'

I must be doing a pretty awful job of hiding my feelings, though, because Marie looks at me sympathetically. 'Maybe they're worried about the baby's heart,' she says.

I am just a step behind her as we walk inside, so I can clearly see the relief on the faces of the parents when they see Marie. 'I understand that you wanted to talk to me, Mr Bauer?' she says.

'That nurse,' Turk says. 'I don't want her touching my son again.'

I can feel heat spreading from the collar of my scrubs up into my scalp. No one likes to be called out in front of her supervisor.

Marie draws herself upright, her spine stiffening. 'I can assure you that Ruth is one of the best nurses we have, Mr Bauer. If there's a formal complaint—'

'I don't want her or anyone who looks like her touching my son,' the father interrupts, and he folds his arms across his chest. He's pushed up his sleeves while I was out of the room. Running from wrist to elbow on one arm is the tattoo of a Confederate flag.

Marie stops talking.

For a moment, I honestly don't understand. And then it hits me with the force of a blow: they don't have a problem with what I've done.

Just with who I am.